Share the Love

SELF-PUBLISH YOUR ROMANCE NOVEL

Full Bloom Publications

FULL BLOOM

For services including consultation and speaking, please contact the publisher.

Full Bloom Publications
Book Writing, Editing, Production, Publishing
Lake of the Ozarks, Missouri
www.FullBloomPublications.com

Book Layout © 2015 BookDesignTemplates.com

Cover design by Claire Crevey

ISBN: 978-1-7326475-0-3
E-book ISBN: 978-1-7326475-1-0

First Edition
Printed in the United States of America

Steps for Self-Publishing Romance Novels

Choose to Self-Publish

THIS BOOK WILL HELP you manage the publication process of your own romance novel. Today, self-publishing is a viable—and for some, more desirable—alternative to traditionally publishing with an established house. There is a lot to consider as you make the decision about which path to pursue, with many factors plus your personal capacity and preferences.

Either way you choose, publishing is an involved process that can last as long as nine months—with a lot to do along the way—so be prepared to engage actively. For many authors, publishing a romance novel is an act of creativity and, while there can be bumps in the road, it is ultimately gratifying to hold the printed book in your hands and know readers are also enjoying it.

Keep in mind that for any author, whether traditionally publishing or self-publishing, the journey to getting your first book to market is the hardest one. After you go through the process once, the next novel will feel much easier because you will know what to expect and do. If you think of the first book as paving the way for more books to follow, you can view your initial effort as a long-term investment in your future.

To help you make the decision about how you want to publish your romance novel, here are some tips about how the business of each option works. While this is not an exhaustive overview of the business, it does offer things to consider that aren't obvious when seeking to publish your romance novel.

At the end of this step, you will find a list of the basic pros and cons of each path to consider as you make the best choice for you.

The Business of Traditional Publishing

Most esteemed romance publishers have closed their doors to authors who want to submit manuscripts directly to them. To filter the pool of potential books, they require that a literary agent submit to them on your behalf. Harlequin is an exception because, while for their bigger publishing programs they require an agent, Harlequin does allow authors to submit directly by uploading manuscripts online.

Literary Agents

A literary agent is an intermediary, who ideally represents your interests in all phases of publication—including contract negotiations, revisions, cover design, any disputes, marketing and publicity, royalty statement reviews, and perhaps your author events—for the duration of your writing career. In exchange, the agent earns a percentage of your royalties, usually 15 percent.

However, that is too often not the reality authors experience with their agents. Many agents are focused on the initial sale of your manuscript to a publishing house. They then drop the ball with everything else—especially their relationship with you since you will naturally want everything they are supposed to offer. The reason for this is that when a traditional publishing house makes an offer to publish your book, it will come with an advance payment. Agents like to try and get this advance as high as they can, mostly because they will receive a percentage of it and this is where they earn most of their money. So they take on more projects with the goal of selling more books rather than managing your interests in an ongoing way. Their time gets overwhelmed by selling efforts so, after the sale, looking out for you gets put on the backburner as something they do in a rushed and haphazard way.

Advance Payments

The truth that many authors barely realize about their advance payment is that it is an advance against their royalties. This means that authors who get an advance will not get paid again until after their book sells enough copies to have earned out that advance. While a large sum of money up front may seem like a big accomplishment, you are actually borrowing against your future earnings.

Royalties

Across various publishing contracts, there are two kinds of royalty structures: gross-sales royalties and net-sales royalties. It used to be that most houses paid gross-sales royalties, which are based on the price of your book. When someone bought your book for $16, you would earn a royalty percentage of that amount as defined in your contract. But these days, the majority of publishers pay net-sales royalties, which subtracts costs—like printing, distribution, and retailer discounts—from the price of your book before royalties are calculated. Sometimes publishers compensate authors for this with a larger percentage for net-sales royalties, but often they do not. This industry transition is not well enough understood by authors, and if a publishing house does its royalty accounting using net-sales, there is really no way of negotiating anything different. And you are not likely to find out which royalty structure they use until the contract is in hand.

Warnings Authors Need to Know

There is a common phenomenon in traditional publishing in which books do not earn out their advance, or come in right at the point that the publishing house budgeted. When this happens, authors do not earn any additional money beyond the advance.

Perhaps what's worse is that when your agent tries to sell your next book to the same publishing house, if that house lost money on your advance, they are less likely to want to work with you again. So you end up either changing publishing houses or receiving lower advances. This follow-up manuscript can even be rejected by everyone, not based on the merits of your writing, but on the sales of your previous book. This has stymied many writing careers and, with an agent pushing for the highest advance possible, you could fall into this trap easily.

Emotional Cost

Trying to break into traditional publishing in the first place is almost guaranteed to be an emotional rollercoaster ride. The process of submitting to agents, hoping for a big book deal with an esteemed publishing house, brings long delays, false hopes, mismatches, and rejections. Then you must find the courage to do it all over again with another agent. Once you finally land an agent, you end up on another rollercoaster as they submit to publishing houses. This process is not for the faint of heart: it requires endurance, fortitude, confidence, and an ability to be humbled over and over again. If you can bounce back from the highs of hopes and the lows of rejections, you may indeed survive the submission process and eventually traditionally publish your romance novel with an esteemed house. If not, self-publishing may be for you.

The Business of Self-Publishing

Self-publishing can be a very positive and lucrative experience when you have a thorough overview and understanding of what it entails, which is what this book provides. It can be more lucrative than traditional publishing, since you keep all profit once you have earned back your initial investment to create and market the book. You are less likely to become a household name, since self-publishing does have some distribution limitations, but that can be overcome by your savvy determination.

Creative Control

Self-publishing gives you control over the project. This is perhaps the biggest benefit of all. Your success is in your hands rather than being affected by the myriad uncontrollable forces at work inside traditional publishing houses. You can avoid the pitfalls that come when, for example, they want a different ending or for you to make significant content changes, a copyeditor changes your meaning or voice, you don't like their cover design, your book is not prioritized highly in the marketing budget, or the editor who acquired your book accepts another job and your project is inherited by a replacement who is lukewarm or indifferent about your novel. So much can happen in the eight-plus months it takes to publish through a traditional house!

While you may not be an expert in editing, design, marketing, publicity, and distribution, you can always research best practices and apply them. Or, if your time is more valuable than the cost of hiring experts to help you, abundant freelancers are now available who are happy to advise you and apply their well-honed skills to your self-publishing endeavor.

Up-Front Costs

With the exception of ongoing promotional and printing costs, most of the money you spend to self-publish your romance novel will be spent up front. So you need to be clear about your up-front budget and your ongoing budget. You can spend a lot, or not that much—it's up to you how much sweat equity you want to put into the project and how much you want to hire help. Costs can range from a thousand dollars to ten thousand or more if you are out to hire the best. You'll read more about this in *Step 5: Learn New Skills or Hire Experts.*

Break-Even Point

It's a great idea to take your budget and determine how many copies you need to sell in order to break even. Here's a way to do it.

1. Set a competitive price through market research into how other romance novels, with similar page counts, in your genre are priced.

2. If you want to sell on Amazon, factor in that they will want a percentage of your money, which can be 40 percent or more. There are calculators online, perhaps through your print-on-demand company, that will let you know how much you will make when you sell a copy of your romance novel on Amazon.

3. You will make more money from direct purchases than from Amazon. To entice readers to buy directly from you, it works in your favor to offer a discount as a reward. Estimate this discount by subtracting 15 to 30 percent from the price.

4. If you decide to print on demand, which is advocated in this book and is discussed in *Step 12: Get Final Files Ready to Print*, it is not an up-front cost. Instead, the cost of printing comes out of the total a reader pays after their purchase. So go ahead and subtract the cost to print one book from the price.

5. Then take your up-front budget total and divide it by the net prices you have calculated for the two scenarios: Amazon sales and direct purchases. This will give you an approximate idea of the number of copies you need to sell in order to break even on your initial investment. As the exact numbers become clearer, you can do this again with more precision.

After you have calculated your break-even point, and know how many copies you need to sell in order to earn a profit, you can take a realistic look at your project and adjust numbers until it strikes you as viable.

Ask yourself the following questions and a strategic approach will begin to take shape.

- Can I realistically reach this many book buyers?
- How long might it take to earn back my up-front investment?
- What promotional efforts are needed to reach these readers?
- If I spend more, or less, than I originally budgeted would I be happier with my break-even point?

You can always return to this calculation as your self-publishing project proceeds. Perhaps you will come in under, or over, what you originally budgeted. Knowing how many books you need to sell before earning profit can help you make course corrections and decisions along the way.

Audience Perception of Self-Published Books

With the right guidance, you can publish a book that only savvy insiders will ever know is self-published. This book will get you far toward accomplishing that, as it offers many things to consider and advice to apply as you go. The truth is that readers don't care nearly as much about big-name publishing brands as writers do. In fact, unless they're hooked on a particular line or series, they care little if at all. They just want to read a good romance story.

So unless you are highly ambitious and feel the need to stamp your own resume with a big-name publisher, there is no need to fear any stigma. If you put effort into having your romance novel edited, designed, and printed so that it meets industry standards, your readers will be happy to purchase it and recommend it.

Making the Decision to Self-Publish

Now that you know more about the businesses of traditional publishing and self-publishing your romance novel, you will be better informed when it comes time to make the commitment to one or the other. It is true that sometimes you can build up such a following and such high sales numbers for your self-published romance novel that you will be approached by (or perhaps you will want to approach) an agent or esteemed traditional publishing house. This can potentially take your success to the next level—or you may prefer to continue to follow the best practices that got you so very far. That's the gift of self-publishing: it's up to you!

Your Choice

How will you publish your romance novel?

❑   Traditionally publish

❑   Self-publish

Traditional Publishing

Pros	Cons
Advance payment	Agent busyness and neglect
Esteemed branding	Agent's cut of your earnings
Expert industry guidance	Breaking-in is an emotional rollercoaster ride
Involves less risk	Little creative control
Potential for agent advocacy	Low royalty percentages
Potential for fame	Many uncontrollable influences

Self-Publishing

Pros	Cons
Amounts of money and effort are up to you	Demands more time
Can hire expert industry guidance	Distribution limitations
Can learn processes and skills	Involves more risk
Complete creative control	Need to pay for guidance along the way
Keep all profit	No advance payment
Less stigma these days	Potential for mistakes
Potentially more lucrative	Requires more effort
Set and manage your own budget	Up-front costs

Write with Love

THE SELF-PUBLISHING JOURNEY BEGINS with the completion of a manuscript. There are many resources that can help you with the elements of a good romance novel, such as plot, characters, setting, conflict, resolution, pacing, and emotional appeal. Make the most of online and in-person offerings as you write, revise, and polish.

No matter how many drafts you have been through in the process of writing your novel, there will come a time to share it with others. If you feel uncertain about whether it is ready, especially if this is your first romance novel, ask yourself the following questions.

- Are my main characters likable?

- Do they overcome internal and external challenges?

- Do they grow as individuals and as a couple?

- Have I done my best to portray things like settings, facts, and time periods accurately and vividly?

- Will readers feel emotionally engaged by the plot and the writing?

- Is there a satisfying sense of resolution at the end?

If you answered yes to all these questions, it may well be time to begin your self-publishing journey. But if there is anything you personally feel you can do better, go ahead and do it. Having a manuscript that is as far along as you can personally take it will work to your benefit, reducing time, money, and hassle along the way. Most writers reach a point where they know they need more feedback to provide reassurance, prompts for more content development, reflections on the writing, and most of all the confidence to move forward with the self-publishing process.

To-Do Checklist

- ❏ Write your romance novel
- ❏ Answer the questions on page 11 to see if you can improve anything yourself
- ❏ Decide it's time to share the novel with others for feedback

Format Your Manuscript

WHEN YOU PREPARE TO share your romance manuscript for any purpose, it's helpful and more efficient to create a formatted version to send along. This step offers tips that will save everyone time, money, and effort.

It's important to distinguish the Microsoft-Word version of the "manuscript" from the fully designed "proof" of your book. The former is used to write and edit your book, and is the topic of this step. The latter is used to lay out and proofread the designed pages of your book in future steps.

Software

Whichever software you used to write your manuscript with, whether Microsoft Word, Scrivener, Google Docs, Apple Pages, or something else, you will generally need to export or convert it into Microsoft Word for your editors and designer. While the merits of various software programs depend on your personal style, the publishing industry runs on Word. Since it is important to hire professionals, you need to use their favored software as you follow the process they recommend to review their work and make suggested changes.

Also, unless you export or convert files, most people cannot open Scrivener, Google Docs, or Pages if they don't have access to it. More people use Microsoft Word, for both PC and Mac, than any other program so it's more likely your manuscript will be readable.

Formatting the Pages

Many authors use their own design senses and visual thought processes to choose how their manuscript looks as they are writing it. This affects things like font choices, font sizes, chapter numbering and titles, section breaks, paragraph indents, line spacing, as well as headers and footers. But if your choices do not reflect universally accepted industry standards, they risk making it more difficult for readers to get used to your style, because it differs from the layout they are accustomed to seeing in most books. It can also cost you money if your editor needs to make these simple formatting changes on your behalf.

Keep in mind that the way a manuscript's pages look is not the way a final, fully designed novel will look. In fact, any excessive formatting in the Microsoft Word version of the manuscript can confuse design programs. Someone will need to simplify and streamline the formatting, so why not you?

Here are the basics for how to format a manuscript.

Font Choice: Serifs are little lines on a font that aid the reader's eyes as they follow a line of text across a page. They are designed to make reading on the page easier, so make the most of them and choose a standard serif font, like Times New Roman, for your manuscript. Sans-serif fonts, or fonts that don't have these little lines on them like Calibri, are better for online and on-screen reading. Choosing a simple font like the two suggested here will help your readers, which is more important than trying to express yourself with a creative font.

Font Size: Even if you write with an enlarged font size, go ahead and change the manuscript so it is set at a 12-point type size. This is standard for readability, and if you want to work at a larger font size you can always zoom in—and so can your readers. Keeping your font at a standard size prevents formatting challenges that come with changing it back and forth between different people.

Chapter Numbering and Titles: Choose whether you want to number your chapters as "Chapter One," "Chapter 1," "One," or even simply "1," and consistently apply your choice to both the table of contents and all your chapter-opening pages. Follow the chapter number with a line break and then offer your chapter title. Go ahead and put both these in bold, and create a couple line breaks beneath them.

Section Breaks: If you have a dingbat, asterisk, or way to indicate a scene change or perhaps a change in the point of view, make it a simple symbol on your keyboard so it easily translates between versions of Microsoft Word. A designer will insert something fancier or more to your liking later.

Paragraph Indents: Because we have become so used to reading online, many people don't think paragraph indents are needed in books either. But paragraph indents are vital visual cues that help readers' eyes move across the page, indicate a pivot point in the content, and identify dialogue. So go ahead and insert paragraph indents, either by manually adding them with the tab button on your keyboard or by selecting the whole manuscript and moving the top arrow on the ruler.

Line Spacing: Single-spaced manuscripts are harder to read. If you are printing hard copies and want people to make corrections or add comments, it's helpful to offer them more space to do so. So select your entire manuscript and double space it.

Header and Footer: For copyright identification and to help out your readers, it's good to create a running header at the top of each manuscript page that offers your name and the title of the book. The running footer should have the page number, especially if you or your reader might print out the manuscript. There's nothing worse than getting pages out of order—and it happens more easily than you might think. So keep everyone straight by making the page number prominent at the bottom of each page. Depending on how you are viewing your document, headers and footers may be invisible on the computer screen but will print out.

Distributing for Critiques

Online piracy is a very real thing. You do not want your manuscript, in uncorrected and unpublished form, to get out into the world. Only email it to trusted readers and professionals, and you may want to state in the body of the email that the manuscript is not to be forwarded or sent electronically for any reason. You can even type "Not for Distribution" on the front page or as a running header or footer.

An editor will need a Word document to work in, and all other readers for critiques will benefit from a printed hard copy or emailed .pdf. This way, they can't accidentally change your writing or formatting. Ask your critique readers whether they want a hard copy snail-mailed or handed to them, or whether they prefer to receive a .pdf electronically for their computer or favorite type of e-reader. By offering your manuscript in their preferred format, they will be more likely to spend their time relating with your romance novel in helpful ways.

To-Do Checklist

- ❑ Convert your manuscript to Microsoft Word
- ❑ Choose to format your own manuscript or to let an editor do it
- ❑ Apply a simple serif or sans-serif font to your manuscript
- ❑ Change all fonts to a 12-point size and zoom in when you want to view it at a larger size
- ❑ Set the numbering style for your chapters and apply it throughout your manuscript
- ❑ Indicate section breaks with a simple keyboard symbol
- ❑ Insert paragraph indents
- ❑ Set the spacing between lines so that it is double-spaced throughout the manuscript
- ❑ Create running headers for the title and your name
- ❑ Create running footers for the page number
- ❑ Mark the manuscript as "Uncorrected Proof—Not for Distribution"
- ❑ Convert to .pdf or print a hard copy to share

Gather Feedback from Readers

EVERY WRITER, EVEN THE most seasoned, can be blind to their own writing. There are things writers neglect to see, and these blind spots can adversely affect your readers' experiences with your romance novel. Whether preliminary readers contribute an idea you didn't think of, correct a fact, point out where they get confused or bored, or call for more details or mood, they will benefit your novel. Preliminary readers may or may not be professionals. They don't even need to be steeped in romance or your particular genre in order to help you out. Humanity shares the storytelling instinct.

So make a list of supportive family and friends who might be willing to read your romance novel and give constructive feedback. You could join a writer's association like Romance Writers of America (RWA), which will pair you with a critique partner. Or attend a writing-critique group that has an uplifted and empowering culture.

By having many preliminary readers, you will be able to gather feedback from a diverse group—which will hopefully get you closer to appealing to a diverse readership once published. Everyone has a different style of reading, with various preferences and critical observations, so getting a fair amount of feedback will not only improve your book, it will also broaden the audience that will ultimately adore your romance novel.

Keep Critiques Positive and Beneficial

It is essential that you only enlist the help of people who are generally supportive of you and your writing effort. The last thing you want is for anyone to crush your inspiration, motivation, belief in yourself, or desire to share your writing with the world. Take anyone who might do that—for whatever selfish reason—off your list. If you attend a toxic-feeling writer's group where there is too much competition, one-upmanship, insensitivity, or putting others down to make themselves look good, do not go back. Their limitations are their own and not yours. Move on without looking back.

Protect your novel from negative influences and only give it to preliminary readers who will honor it enough to help make it better. If you suspect that your circle will do more harm than good, it will be worth it to pay a professional romance reader who can write you a report with recommendations.

Direct Your Readers' Feedback

Especially if your preliminary readers are not used to critiquing, it is very helpful to direct their feedback. This can be done in a cover letter that you distribute with a hard copy or in the body of the email that attaches your manuscript. You can ask for specific help with aspects of the novel you struggled with or suspect are weak. Or you can share these general questions that prompt readers' thoughts as they progress through the novel.

- Do sentences flow well?

- Do you feel carried along by the story?

- Identify where the writing feels off somehow, whether too descriptive, curt, sparse, detailed, fast-moving, slow-moving, or at all confusing

- Do you ever get lost, unable to follow what is happening?

- When do you get bored?

- Are any facts or details incorrect?

- Is the setting, or world in which the story takes place, vivid enough?

- Do you have specific ideas for improving a scene?

- Is any important information about a character left out?

- Do you like and care about the characters?

- What else would you like to know about a character?

- What scenes do you find gripping, when you can't put the book down?

- What are the emotional effects of different scenes?

- Do you want to feel more drawn in to specific scenes than you were?

- Is the resolution satisfying?

As you can see, preliminary readers are doing much more than reading for typos and spelling errors—though identifying those can definitely be helpful. You want your readers to dive into the story and apply their discerning minds. If it helps, instruct them to imaginatively put themselves in the place of your ideal romance readership rather than reading from their own genre preferences. This can work out well if you appeal to humanity's common love for storytelling, even if your readers personally prefer nonfiction or literary fiction.

When you send your romance manuscript to readers, include instructions for how you would like them to offer their comments. If they are relating with a hard copy, request that they use a colored pen so their notes will stand out to you better: purple and green work great, as blue doesn't quite stand out enough and red can feel harsh when you are reviewing their marked-up pages. If they are reading on-screen via a .pdf, most software will offer a sticky-note function so they can post comments throughout the electronic version of your manuscript.

Make the Most of Feedback

When you receive feedback on your romance novel, you are almost guaranteed to feel a sting. Prepare yourself for this, and for how you will overcome the sting and get to work making your romance novel better. Because if you are only looking for praise, you can't improve. People are not actually helping you when they: express their love for you only through praise, fear making you angry, want to protect you from criticism, or just want to make you happy. They are hindering you.

The best readers will offer comments that you can use productively. Even if a reader simply writes in the margins "I'm bored here" or "I don't get it," that's valuable feedback! It means you can enliven or clarify a scene. You can get creative with your writing to bolster areas that readers identified as needing improvement. And if more than one reader identifies the same problem spot, you can thank your lucky stars that you can now apply your skill to making your novel as great as it can be.

The key to overcoming the sting of critiques is gratitude. Feel thankful to the reader for giving your romance novel so much time, attention, and personal engagement. They clearly care and want to help you make it better. And in turn, you can care enough to take their feedback seriously.

That's not to say you must incorporate every single recommendation or comment. The beauty of self-publishing is that this is still your book—no one has enough leverage over you to force a change or edit. So keep a balanced mindset as you consider reader feedback to weigh what you want to accomplish with your novel against ways readers are calling for improvement. There is a balance there, and while it may take a lot of thinking through and a couple more drafts of some scenes, you will feel it when your romance novel is really shining.

To-Do Checklist

- ❏ Make a list of supportive friends and family
- ❏ Join a writer's association
- ❏ Attend a writing-critique group
- ❏ Protect your novel from negative influences
- ❏ Direct your readers' feedback
- ❏ Give instructions for sharing comments
- ❏ Overcome the sting that comes with feedback through gratitude
- ❏ Decide which recommendations to pursue
- ❏ Work creatively to improve your novel

Learn New Skills or Hire Experts

As readers are reviewing your manuscript, make the most of the window of time and plan your self-publishing process. You will have already set your budget, so now consider how you will spend it. The tasks you do not hire out, and decide to do yourself, will lower your up-front costs but to many people the time these tasks take up is also valuable. So consider what your time is worth to you—it may save you money to hire an expert. At the same time, once you learn new skills with your first self-published novel, you can apply them to future books. So read on to learn more about project management, editing, cover design, interior-pages design, and e-book conversion so that you can make an informed decision to DIY or to hire.

Project Management

Someone needs to run the show. This can be you or it can be a consultant, project manager with knowledge of book publishing, or someone who is known inside publishing houses as a production editor. If you have a long vision for many self-published romance novels, you may want to consider hiring someone to help you with your first book. You'll learn a lot along the way, which you can then apply yourself to future books.

Here is what project management for a self-publishing project involves, with pros and cons of both DIY and hiring an expert.

Hiring a Team of Freelancers

There are many websites where freelancers have profiles with portfolios of their work. You can post a job and they will apply. Their work is often reviewed by others who have hired them, so in a way you get to check references. But this is still a bit of a shot in the dark. A project manager, consultant, or production editor will come with a proven lineup of freelancers who they have worked with before, who they know produce quality finished products, and who are enjoyable to engage along the way.

Scheduling Due Dates

It is essential to create and maintain a schedule of due dates for every step in the process. You will need to set a publication date that you will base your promotional efforts around, and then work backward to create your schedule. As a very general rule that will need to be adapted for holidays, travel, cramped workloads, and life events, allocate at least two weeks for every stage. You will need to run different schedules for your manuscript, cover, and interior-pages proofs, allow time for the printer to prepare your files, and build in the e-book conversion.

Here is a sample schedule that covers all the steps that happen on the way to having printed copies in hand no later than October 15th. This book you are reading covers all these steps—although right now the language may seem like code. But once you have read through this book and are familiar with book-publishing vocabulary, you will understand every step.

Manuscript

    Manuscript to content-development editor: April 1
    Content edit Round 1 to author review: May 1
    Author review of content edit to Round 2: May 15
    Content edit Round 2 delivery: June 1
    Manuscript to copyeditor: June 4
    Copyedited manuscript to author review: June 30
    Author review of copyedits to corrections: July 15
    Copyedited manuscript delivery: June 28

Cover

    Front cover mockups to author review: June 25
    Final front cover approval: July 9
    Cover copy to author review: August 9
    Author changes to cover copy: August 16
    Cover copy to designer: August 17
    ISBN and Barcode to designer: August 17
    Cover design to Proof 1: August 30
    Proof 1 corrections to designer: September 13
    Cover design to Proof 2: September 20
    Cover design for final approval: September 27
    Final files uploaded to on-demand printer: October 1

Interior-Pages Proofs

    Copyedited manuscript to Design 1: June 28
    Interior sample layout to author for review: August 2
    Author approval of sample layouts: August 9
    Designed interior to Proof 1: August 16
    Proof 1 corrections to Design 2: August 30
    Corrected proof to Proof 2: September 13
    Final corrections to Design 3: September 20
    Designed interior for final approval: September 27
    Final files uploaded to on-demand printer: October 1

E-book Conversion

    September

Delivery of Printed Books

    October 10

When you hire freelancers, you will need to have their due dates at the ready to make sure they will be available when you need them. Notice that there are also due dates for tasks you, as the author, need to meet so that at every phase you can review and offer feedback on freelancer work.

Sending the Right Versions of Files to the Right People

Put a version-control system to work for you. Getting the right version of your files to the right person is absolutely essential. Otherwise, once you catch the goof, you will need to completely redo all your work or the freelancer will need to. Don't rely on email dates or messages to orient people to the version and the intended work. Don't rely on someone else's personal organization system, especially if they work on multiple projects. And don't assume others will be able to interpret your personal system. All those things can go disastrously wrong. So label every file with the title of your book, what the file contains, the intended task, and the date you are sending it out. Here are four examples for various phases.

- Love Is Here_copyedited manuscript_to copyedit corrections_11.15.18

- Love Is Here_final manuscript_to design for flowing_11.15.18

- Love Is Here_cover illustration_author comments_11.15.18

- Love Is Here_interior pages_to proof 1_11.15.18

When you receive files back from someone who does not follow your file-management system, perhaps having changed your file name to work within their own personal organization, be sure to change the file name straightaway when saving it. And do not simply replace your master copy—you will benefit down the road from having a complete record of every stage of the self-publishing journey. A solid file-management system will ensure you have all the files you need, labeled exactly as you need them to be, anytime you might need them.

Managing Invoices

You will need to negotiate terms of payment when you hire a freelancer. You can simply ask them what their preferred payment structure is, or you can propose the one you favor. Freelancers will either work for an hourly rate or a flat fee, which is an agreed-upon total that covers all phases up to your final approval and their final delivery, or for an hourly rate.

Flat Fee: Illustrators and designers may work for a flat fee, which makes their time management up to them. It covers everything up until the point that you are happy with their work, which might be an advantage to you if there ends up being a lot of revision. If you are hiring through an online freelancer website, you can post the amount you budget for this phase and anyone applying will be willing to complete the work for that fee. Keep in mind that if you lowball your fee you may get applicants, but not from people with the talent and skillset for truly quality work. So look at similar jobs others are posting and assess what a fair flat fee is. You can also choose your ideal freelancers and message them with a project description, asking them what they would charge to do it. Usually, to get started on the project, the freelancer will want half of the flat-fee total paid up front and then the other half will be paid on completion of the project.

Hourly Rate: Content editors, copyeditors, and proofreaders tend to work at hourly rates. The best measure of a fair hourly rate, by which you are more likely to get quality work, is the online rate sheet maintained by the Editorial Freelancers Association (EFA). Rates are open to negotiation and, if you have a budget that you want to stick to, definitely tell the freelancer what that is and see if they are willing to work within it. You can also send your manuscript or the .pdf of your proof (which is the fully designed pages) to the potential freelancer to get a time estimate. Everyone works at different speeds, and if you are hiring professionals they will be able to say things like: they are slower than others, but thorough, so the additional money is worth it; they work fast with an eye for details; or they can tell from your sample that the work will go either swiftly or take a real hands-on approach (which is one way of saying you will need a lot of their help). Freelancers working at an hourly rate may want a payment structure in which they send you an invoice with each round that is completed, once they have accumulated a certain number of hours, or some may even wait to be paid until the project is complete (this is rare, but it does happen).

Once you receive an invoice from a freelancer, you generally have 30 days to pay them. This can help you juggle your cash flow, but remember that if this is an initial invoice or a midway invoice, paying a freelancer swiftly will help motivate them to continue to do terrific work for you. And paying them straight-away upon delivery of the completed project is a great way to say thank you and maintain an ongoing, positive relationship that can stretch far into your future of self-publishing romance novels.

Giving Instruction and Feedback to Designers

The look and feel of your self-published romance novel is the first thing readers will encounter. If the designs of both the cover and the interior pages don't look familiar to what they are used to seeing from the big-name publishers—if they seem sloppy, haphazard, or amateur—then your novel may get judged negatively in an instant and they will not buy it. Why take that risk? This kind of quality control is something a consultant may be able to help you with, since they have managed many book-publishing projects and navigated all types of designs.

Book cover design and layout takes a refined eye, an understanding of what appeals to your market, and knowledge of your content. Sometimes a little tweak can make a profound difference. Yes, you can learn these things through research and market awareness, and you may have an innate talent for artistic composition, color, and font choice. You can also gather feedback from family and friends to help you refine a design. You will read more about this in *Step 6: Envision Your Cover*. Consider the benefit a consultant might contribute to this essential part of a successfully self-published romance novel.

Keeping Things Moving Toward the Publication Date

The person who is acting as project manager for your self-publishing journey, whether that is you or someone you hire, will need to do things like:

- Keep up on correspondence
- Answer questions from freelancers
- Give clear creative direction
- Send check-ins to keep things on schedule
- Adjust the schedule when life interrupts it
- Email electronic versions
- Snail-mail hardcopy proofs
- Approach potential endorsers

Some things that a hired project manager can contribute are pretty tough to offer yourself. These include reassurance when things get complicated or messy, the confidence that comes with professional experience, and answers to your own questions along the way. Some authors find it's worth it to pay to have their hands held throughout the process, to only relate with one person instead of a team of people, and to know that they don't need to fear errors or mistakes that could slip by them out of pure innocence.

Editing

While the term "editing" is a catch phrase, there are so many different types of editors who all specialize in a specific style of editing. This is a fairly comprehensive list so that you will never again say "my editor" casually, but will instead speak with precision.

Acquisitions Editor: The person in a publishing house who purchases manuscripts from agents and acts as the author's central point-person

Book Doctor: Offers a very thorough edit, or even rewrite, to solve problems in manuscripts that authors can't fix themselves—for whatever reason

Content-Development Editor: Offers prompts, queries, and feedback on manuscripts so authors can revise to bolster the story and its plot, characters, flow, pacing, resolution, ending, and more

Copyeditor: Corrects grammar, typos, spelling, and passive voice to ensure that writing is up to industry standards

Line Editor: Helps sentences flow better, read more effortlessly, and capture intended emotions

Production Editor: Coordinates the production process, including the team of freelancers who copyedit and proof-read, and liaises with the designer

Proofreader: Scrubs the fully designed cover and interior pages clean of any remaining errors

In your self-publishing project, you will likely only need to relate with content-development editing, copyediting, and proof-reading. If you do end up with very useful feedback from your preliminary readers, you just might be able to forgo content-development editing—but it is highly recommended that you hire someone to do it anyway. You will absolutely need to hire the copyeditor and proofreader. No author should attempt to correct their own writing, for these reasons.

- You can have blind spots that keep you from seeing problems
- There are going to be standard industry rules you are not aware of or do not know
- You may have read the novel so many times you experience "reader fatigue" and cannot see it objectively
- You are too close, or attached, to the material to be objective

Editing is not the place to pinch pennies—it is your best investment. When you consider who to hire, look at the genre or type of book that potential editors specialize in and try to match their background with your romance novel. This is most important for a content-development editor, but a copyeditor who specializes in nonfiction for example may—however well-intentioned —destroy the voice or storytelling in a novel and may not handle dialogue as well. Someone with a lot of experience with romance novels may contribute wonderful surprises from their bag of accumulated tricks. Proofreaders, on the other hand, can come from any genre or field since their contribution comes more from their alert attention, keen eyes, ability to spot errors however subtle, and knowledge of style-guide rules.

Every editor you hire must be versed in, and use, the most recent edition of the *Chicago Manual of Style,* which is a massive volume of rules that the book industry uses to maintain consistency and best practices. In fact, one of the biggest advantages of hiring editing professionals is that they know the rules, so that you don't need to.

Cover Design

Cover design is creative and fun, and some authors begin to visualize what they would like on their covers before the writing is even complete. That is great—and encouraged. It is essential to gather your ideas for the front and back cover, which you'll learn about more in *Step 6: Envision Your Cover.*

Graphic Designer

It might be tempting to think that you can go ahead and design your cover yourself. Unless you have been trained as a graphic designer, and have intimate working knowledge of software like Adobe's Photoshop, Illustrator, and InDesign, as well as an understanding of stock-photo licensing, it is a good idea to hire a professional designer.

Graphic designers like to say they can design anything, and some can, but as you check out their portfolios look for examples of their book covers to see if you like what they create. It may be well worth it to hire someone with book-industry experience.

Downloadable Template

If you just want a nice, professionally designed cover, and are not that picky about what's on it—or are in possession of a high-resolution stock photo with the right license that you know you want to use—you can use a downloadable book cover template. These templates have been created by graphic designers, and online there are many styles and moods to choose from.

Illustrator

While a graphic designer may be able to capture the mood of your romance novel by searching the extensive online databases of stock images, which include photographs and other artistic media, you might want to customize your cover. You can hire an illustrator to work in any style or medium, such as digital, pastel, colored pencil, or ink. They can convey the exact look and presence of your main characters or capture a certain type of drama, landscape, symbol, or scene.

Illustrators are more affordable than you might think, since there are so many wonderfully talented people who enjoy doing it. You will need to be prepared to give them clear creative direction, with as much precision as possible, so they can create the results you're looking for. Don't assume anything about their creativity—if you want a certain look and feel, put it in writing for them in detail as you will learn to do in Step 6. Send them photographs to use as models for what they will draw. Choose the colors you want.

They will send you sketches to review and offer feedback on. Then more detailed, color versions will follow. Working with an illustrator can be fun and collaborative, just do remember to communicate your feedback and changes with kindness.

Keep in mind that while the illustrator will give you the custom image you want, you will likely still need to hire a graphic designer to choose fonts for the title, author name, and back-cover copy, and place them in just the right way.

Photographer and Models

Hiring a photographer with a studio and models to represent your main characters is definitely an option, but a very expensive one. It is so cost prohibitive that it is not recommended for a self-published novel, unless you have studio photography experience, personally know people who have the right looks and are photogenic enough to act as models, can fill makeup and wardrobe needs, and can work with images in Adobe Photoshop. Photo shoots can be great fun, so if this is the path for you, enjoy the process. If not, go ahead and search the vast online archives of stock photos available for licensing to see if you can find one that captures what you're looking for. You can always send the link to your graphic designer.

As you hire the type of help you want for your cover design, remember that there is more to a cover than the front. While that is the most eye-catching part, you will also need help creating a spine that can stand out on a bookshelf, and a back cover that is engaging visually but leaves room for sales copy (the interest-grabbing summary on the back of the book), any endorsements you want to solicit, an author bio, and a barcode. Include all of this in your creative direction for anyone you hire who does not have book-design experience.

Interior-Pages Design

You may be able to find one designer to do both your cover and your interior-pages designs. This could add a sense of continuity between the exterior and interior of your romance novel, but there are other ways to do this, as you'll learn in *Step 9: Flow Your Interior Pages.*

The interior-pages design process has been simplified by the availability of great templates you can use. If you have the time, a desire to learn new skills, and an eye for details, this is something you can do yourself. But if you are lacking in any of those three areas, definitely hire a freelancer.

The tasks involved in designing your own interior pages include the following, which you will also learn more about in Step 9.

- Flowing the text into a template
- Making adjustments to accommodate lengths of paragraphs and chapters
- Correcting awkward word breaks and stacked words
- Accurately inputting corrections from the proofreader and yourself into the file
- Creating a print-ready final file

Romance novels have very clean, simple layouts, so for a self-published romance novel you could create a great-looking interior yourself. Don't start from scratch—downloadable book design templates are very inexpensive and will save you a lot of trial-and-error distress. Locate a few websites and search their inventory for the style, fonts, and look that appeal to you. The templates are designed for use in software like Microsoft Word, Apple Pages, and Adobe InDesign—depending on what you can access. They come with instructions for flowing your text into the template, refining it, and correcting formatting errors. Some can even be used to convert your final proof into e-book formats.

E-Book Conversion

E-book conversion to all formats—including a .mobi file for Kindle readers and an .epub file for all other readers including mobile phones—is quite affordable. So unless you really want to fill your time and learn a new skill, it might be best to hire a freelancer to do this. However, because romance novels have such clean and straightforward interiors, with the help of an interior-pages template or even free conversion through e-book distributors, this is absolutely something you can do yourself.

Sales Copy

It truly is a fine art to write attention-grabbing sales copy for the back of your book and for online store webpages. Not only does it need to draw interest, it needs to do so in a small amount of space. This is why it is a great idea to hire a copywriter to do this for you, especially one familiar with the romance market. So even if you write a great promotional paragraph or two, run it by a professional copywriter to have them punch it up and increase your novel's appeal.

This step has hopefully not only helped you prepare for what you will do and for who you will hire to help you, it has also offered a high-level overview of the self-publishing process. The steps to come go more in depth with each phase, offering you things to consider and also tips for avoiding common mistakes, to create a market-ready romance novel.

Your Learning and Hiring Plan

Who will manage the publishing process?

❑ Me

❑ An expert at _____ flat or hourly rate

Have you budgeted to hire the following editors?

❑ Content-development editor at_____flat or hourly rate

❑ Copyeditor at _____ hourly rate

❑ Proofreader at _____ hourly rate

Who will design your cover?

❑ Me

❑ Graphic designer at _____ flat rate

❑ Illustrator at _____ flat rate

Who will lay out your interior pages?

❑ Me

❑ Graphic designer at _____ flat or hourly rate

Who will convert to e-book?

❑ Me

❑ Conversion company at _____ flat rate

Who will write or hone sales copy for the cover and online promotion?

❑ Me

❑ Copywriter at _____ flat or hourly rate

List of things you need to learn how to do:

_____

_____

_____

_____

_____

Total estimated cost of hiring expert help: _____

Envision Your Cover

ENVISIONING YOUR OWN COVER is one of the best parts of self-publishing your romance novel, because publishing houses don't hand over much creative control to authors. You may already have ideas for your cover. If not, now is the perfect time to look at other covers to see what styles you admire that capture the tone of your novel. Here are some ideas for you to consider for using characters, setting, architecture, animals, vehicles, symbols, colors, type treatments, and series consistency to convey your romance story visually.

Characters

- Many romance covers feature the main characters, who can be sensually or innocently engaged with each other
- Others feature one character, whether female or male, depending on how you want to grab attention
- Some are featured in part, or through details, so that the characters' looks are left up to the reader's imagination and your descriptive writing
- Costumes for historical romances are very enticing, and evoke the period you are writing about
- Paranormal romances might feature characters' appearances, powers, or costumes from the world you have built

Setting

- Whether your novel is set in the city, country, or suburbs, having a sense of the setting on the cover can set a tone and grab the attention you're looking for

- A specific and identifiable landscape can lend a sense of place and also set a tone, whether redwoods on the California coast, skyscrapers of Manhattan, hay-baled hills of Iowa, dramatic Rocky Mountains in Wyoming, or great plains of Texas

- Weather can create a serene mood, a sense of drama or anticipation, a hint at challenges to be overcome, an uplifting feeling of inspiration, or anything else you can imagine

- The sky offers a terrific open space where you can place your title, so consider what kind of clouds or sunrise/midday/sunset colors and views come with your setting

Architecture

- A house is a popular feature on romance novel covers, with architecture that sets the time period, location, and mood

- If important scenes take place at a certain type of building, like an office, penthouse, barn, hospital, or church, putting it on the cover can convey a lot to readers

Animals

- Pets can be characters that readers come to care about, so a cat, dog, horse, or any other animal from the story makes a great cover feature

- An animal can convey the personality of one of your main characters, so if you have compared him or her to a tiger, fox, stallion, lone wolf, or spider weaving a web, for example, consider putting the animal on your cover

Vehicles

- Like architecture, a vehicle can set the time period, place, and mood
- If an important scene involves travel, a car chase, or takes place on a boat, train, or airplane, including this on your cover can lend a taste of what's inside

Symbols

- An enticing detail from your novel can symbolize the central conflict in the story, like a key in a lock, a necklace pendant, a leaf, a river, a piece of clothing, some object belonging to one of the main characters, the very thing that has gone missing, or a significant clue encountered along the way

Colors

- The palette and shades that you put on your cover will go a long way toward capturing a mood and setting a tone
- If a color is significant to your story, consider making it dominant on your cover
- Often certain colors are commonly associated with places or landscapes—such as turquoise for New Mexico, dark green for evergreen forests in Oregon, purple for a magical world, or black for outer space—and readers will appreciate the familiar cue

- A very dominant color can create a clear mood, however the direction that you take the mood in depends on the rest of your design—for example, red can indicate desire, danger, urgency, blood, and so much more

Type Treatments

- You may want the title to be the most significant thing about your cover—if so, you will want it big and the font you choose will be extremely important

- Font is as expressive as any picture, and choosing the right one is a real art form in itself, so you might want to research font designs

- If you want to build your author brand more than anything else, consider putting your name at the top of the cover or making it larger than the title

Series Consistency

- If your romance novel is part of a series, you will want to put the name of the series in a consistent place—and in an identical style—on all covers of novels in that series so it takes readers only a glance to recognize it

- Brainstorm ways to bring continuity to the series covers, for example hire the same illustrator to create all the covers in the same style and medium, think of symbols that run throughout the series, or if all the novels involve the same main character have him or her doing different things specific to each novel

Because the sky truly is the limit with your romance novel cover, spend a lot of time mulling over your options and prioritizing them. You can't put everything on your cover, in fact, simple is powerful. Write down your ideas. Then reread them, close your eyes, and visualize each one.

You can pay your illustrator or graphic designer to create a collection of sample sketches or mockups, in black and white or in color, to help you better visualize the options. Create a creative-direction description for each "concept" and then when you see several of them side by side, you can begin to mix and match elements across them to get closer to your ideal cover.

Giving Creative Direction

When you can convey your cover vision to your illustrator or graphic designer with clarity, precision, detailed descriptions, and examples, you will save a lot of time, money, and stress. It truly is more up to you to communicate your creative direction clearly than it is up to the freelancer to just get it. Their understanding depends on how specific you are. Sure, they can and will contribute creative ideas along the way—and you want them to. But the overall concept that they are shooting for needs to come from you. So you will want to give them clear creative direction. Here are all the things your illustrator or graphic designer needs to know before they begin work. You will find instructions and examples in parentheses.

- **Novel title** (along with your idea for its placement in the design)
- **Series title** (if there is one, along with your idea for its placement in the design)
- **Author name or pen name** (along with your idea for its placement in the design)
- **Time period or world** (be descriptive if it's not immediately recognizable or you made it up)
- **Brief description of the plot** (this is handy to have ready at any time, so do put in some effort—at some point—to write a one-paragraph description of your plot)

- **Trim size** (the standard trim size is 6" x 9" for both the front cover and back cover, so you will need to lay out a 12" x 9" cover plus spine width—which you can calculate through your printer)

- **Bleed** (this is the amount that the cover image needs to "bleed" over the edges of the cover to aid printing processes—you can get the exact measurement needed from your printer)

- **Medium** (photograph, digital, pastel, acrylic, watercolor, ink)

- **Style** (life-like, textured, line art, silhouetted)

- **Mood** (dark and moody, bright and inspiring, fantastical, mysterious)

- **Colors** (also describe how bright, earth-toned, dark, or contrasting the shades of these colors should be)

- **Characters** (don't require your freelancer to read your book for a sense of this, instead describe important features like age, hair and eye color, and include what is important to emphasize about them—inner strength, an Adam's apple, muscles, sweet expression with full lips, cowboy hat, curly hair, playful disposition—even offering example photographs of people who convey the poise and looks you need)

- **Setting** (offer a description of the setting and example photographs that capture it well)

- **Themes** (to stir your freelancer's creativity, share some of the major themes of the novel and see what they come up with to convey them)

- **Anything else they will benefit from** (such as font preferences, sample covers that you love from other authors, graphic layout ideas, or composition ideas)

Reviewing Works in Progress

Allow the professional illustrator or graphic designer to manage the process by which you work. Generally, they will send you preliminary ideas to review, consider, give feedback on, and choose between. These can be rough works, so have no fear, the faults will likely be tended to and fixed as the drafts progress.

You may be lucky to be struck by a preliminary idea and know "This is the one!" Or you may want to combine aspects of different ideas. Feel free to invite the freelancer to head in a certain direction and play with it more.

Once you have chosen the basic layout and main images, details will start emerging that the freelancer will want your feedback on to ensure they are on track. This includes character or landscape features, costume designs, various stock images, and colors.

When you give feedback to an illustrator or graphic designer, remember that—like you—the freelancer is a creative person who, while a professional, is still an artist who wants their work to be appreciated. It's good practice to first tell them, whether via email or on the phone, what you love about what they did and what they got right. This sets an overall positive tone and the message that things are heading in the right direction—even if they're not quite there yet.

When it comes time to talk about what you want them to change, make sure the feedback is specific, directive, and action-oriented. The goal is that after hearing your change requests, the freelancer will know exactly what they can do to meet your needs. Here are some examples of how to phrase change requests.

- "Rose is looking too young. Can you age her ten years? She directs a team in a corporation, so she needs that kind of leadership poise."

- "Please lighten the whole mood by about 20 percent. This is more terrifying than the suspense I'm going for and I think I get that impression because the wolf is so vicious-looking. Maybe it would feel lighter if he wasn't snarling."

- "That's not quite the right shade of purple. I'll locate the exact shade I want and send it to you."

- "On second thought, the original composition is beginning to look too cluttered. Can we remove half the bubbles?"

What it all comes down to is that both you and the freelancer want you to be happy with the cover! So keep working together to meet that common goal. Sticking with a positive, collaborative tone when communicating changes will save so much heartache and stress on all sides that you may truly enjoy the sense of teamwork. And you never know when their creativity will completely delight you.

Workflow Tips

You can work with your cover illustrator or graphic designer in an ongoing way that overlaps with the editing process for your manuscript. Just be sure to set a completion date that:

- Works for both of your schedules

- Will have your front cover completed in time for your promotional efforts to begin well in advance of the publication date

- Makes the font selection before the interior-design pages are created—if you want the cover fonts to also be in the interior pages as chapter titles (not required, but certainly a nice idea to provide readers with consistency)

Your cover is now underway, and you can return your creative energy to working on your manuscript with professional editorial assistance.

To-Do Checklist

- ❑ Envision your cover
- ❑ Give detailed creative direction
- ❑ Review concept mock-ups
- ❑ Choose a concept
- ❑ Time the workflow
- ❑ Review progress and give specific, directive, and action-oriented feedback

Bolster with Content-Development Editing

YOU TOOK THE MANUSCRIPT as far as you could on your own with the help of your preliminary readers. Now you will benefit from professional guidance. Content-development editors have a true knack for empathically putting themselves in the place of your ideal reader, who you are writing for, and your target audience. This is particularly true if they specialize in romance novels.

Once you send them your manuscript, you never know what kind of feedback you will receive. Rest assured that they will be watching out for ways to improve these things, among others.

- Believability
- Chapter structure
- Chapter titles
- Character development
- Clarity
- Dialogue
- Emotional appeal

- Flow
- Length
- Pacing
- Plot development
- Resolution
- Story progression
- Vividness

Working with a Content-Development Editor

Because your editor is a professional, they will have a process they either prefer to follow or that they think will best fit your needs and your manuscript's needs. It's a good idea to follow their recommendations. This section will give you an idea of what to expect along the way.

Editing in Rounds

One round of editing consists of two phases: the editor's work on the manuscript and then your work to revise the manuscript. The editor may want to work on one chapter, and then send it to you to work on—which is a good way of working in tandem, especially if you are on a rushed publishing schedule. Or the editor may prefer to work on the entire manuscript for a defined amount of time, and then send it to you to work on for another defined period. This way of working will benefit elements that span the entire novel, like plot and character development.

Either way, you will receive edited files that you can expect to put time, energy, and inspiration into revising according to the editor's prompts and recommendations. You may choose to have the editor read your work again once you are finished with that round—in fact, you can do as many rounds as you need and can afford. It is beneficial to at least do a second round so they can confirm that you answered their queries and prompts, and that you successfully met their suggestions and recommendations. You may also appreciate getting a formal green light that your manuscript content is fully developed and ready for copyediting.

Editing with Computer Software

Your editor will almost certainly work using Microsoft Word's tracked-changes function. You will learn how to work with these changes in depth in *Step 8: Smooth Grammar with Copyediting*. Basically, this function allows your editor to highlight passages they want to comment on in the right-hand margin of your document. These "comment bubbles" can be replied to or deleted as you address each issue. Your editor will also likely make changes to the text directly, and everything they do is tracked in a color, in this way.

- Inserted text is underlined

- Deleted text is crossed out

- Moved text is double-underlined (unless they cut and paste, which is marked like inserted text)

- Formatting changes are identified in the right-hand margin

Depending on your editor's preference, they may ask you to also track your own changes when it is your turn to work on the manuscript. That way, they can check your changes without reading the entire novel again. If they request this, see Step 8 for more on using the function.

On the other hand, the content-development editor may want you to go ahead and accept their edits, which you approve of, appreciate, or see the need for. They may want you to work without tracked changes so that they can read your novel through again and gather fresh thoughts rather than revisiting their previous thoughts.

Either way, you may want to keep a complete record of your back and forth with them. If so, go ahead and track all your own changes, saving that as a unique version. You can work with a clean view so that you do not get distracted by all the colors, but Microsoft Word will be tracking everything in the background. You do this by clicking on the Review tab at the top of your screen and selecting "All Markup" or "No Markup" from a drop-down menu.

More on this in *Step 8: Smooth Grammar with Copyediting.*

Editorial Letters

In addition to marking your manuscript with comments and changes, an editor is likely to write an editorial letter to you. This is a document or cover email that gives you an overview of their work and recommendations. It helps to pull their specific comments in the manuscript together into a big-picture view of what you need to do. It also can offer helpful tips, encouragement, and publication ideas. The tone should be supportive enough to help you through the emotional waves that come to most authors when reading editorial feedback.

Holding Up in the Midst of Feedback

A professional editor should be skilled in the way they deliver content-development feedback so that you know they enjoyed your book and that their recommendations are meant to help you make your book even more enjoyable for readers. Just because they have edits and ideas to contribute does not mean you have failed to write a terrific book. All writers of any genre benefit from professional feedback.

You would go through this same process if you were publishing with a traditional house, only you would have less choice in how you respond to edits. Hopefully, your editor will explain their reasoning behind the larger edits and recommendations so that you come to perceive the need for them and even appreciate how following the guidance will benefit your romance novel.

At the same time, this is your self-publishing endeavor, so you have given yourself mighty veto power. If you feel, for any reason, that an edit or idea compromises some element of your book, you can reject the edit, perhaps explain your reasoning for doing so in a comment bubble, and move on. The benefit is that you have made this decision consciously, rather than out of ignorance, and know full well why you are not following the editor's recommendation. This is a form of empowerment that authors who traditionally publish rarely feel they can exercise.

Once the light is green to indicate that you have fully developed your novel's content, either the editor or you will prepare a clean version of the manuscript (without any tracked changes or comment bubbles) to transmit to the copyeditor for your next level of editing.

To-Do Checklist

- ❑ Establish a process
- ❑ Send your manuscript to the content-development editor
- ❑ Learn the basics of editing with Microsoft Word tracked-changes function
- ❑ Review the edits
- ❑ Veto anything you disagree with
- ❑ Respond to prompts and queries
- ❑ Revise as needed
- ❑ Send revised manuscript back to the editor
- ❑ Go through as many rounds as needed
- ❑ Receive a green light indicating that your content is fully developed

Smooth Grammar with Copyediting

AT THIS POINT, CONGRATULATIONS for completing a fully developed romance novel! You have worked hard, reread and revised your manuscript many times, taken feedback seriously as something that can help you create a more enjoyable reading experience, and managed to get through the biggest emotional challenges that you will face on your journey of self-publishing. It is now time to iron out any remaining wrinkles.

Some authors wonder why one editor can't accomplish all levels of editing at once. As you can now appreciate, each editor along the way needs to maintain a different type of focus. At this point, you too will shift your focus from the big picture to the details as you work with a copyeditor.

It is essential for you to accept that the content is complete and resist the temptation to revise or rewrite beyond considering the copyeditor's changes and queries. Doing so will disrupt the process and cost you more time and money to iron the wrinkles from whatever you change.

So take a deep breath and change the lens through which you view the manuscript so that you only see details.

Industry Guidelines

Sometimes your copyeditor will make changes to your manuscript that can seem so minor, you may wonder why they're
needed. Book publishing is a precise industry. It adheres to a
massive volume of style requirements known as the *Chicago
Manual of Style*, which outlines grammar rules and best-practice
standards. As you review the copyeditor's work, know that they
are following these extensive guidelines as well as their own keen
eye for ways to subtly improve writing. Changes can be as small
as removing a comma or breaking up a long sentence into more
succinct statements. Unlike your content-development editor,
a copyeditor will not be able to explain their reasoning behind
changes. Instead, have confidence that you hired a professional.

Stylesheet

If your copyeditor needs to make any decisions that are specific
to your book, especially if there are foreign words, intentional
misspellings, capitalization choices, or styles in your writing
like dialect that need to be preserved, the copyeditor will record
them in a stylesheet. You will have the opportunity to review
this stylesheet when you review the copyedited manuscript. The
stylesheet will eventually be sent to the proofreader, who will
refer to it in order to ensure that everything they notice as odd
or unique has been done intentionally as a part of the book's
established style.

Permissions

A professional copyeditor should include advising you on seeking
any necessary permissions, or revising so that you don't need to
seek permission, as part of their work. If they do not mention it
in your preliminary negotiation, be sure to confirm that they will
keep their eyes out for any permission concerns, point them out
to you, and advise you.

Generally, you will need to seek permission to reprint anything that is the intellectual property of someone else. This includes lines of poetry and song lyrics, which are the two most common things that romance writers like to quote. There is a vague aspect of copyright law known as "fair use," which allows some works to be quoted, reprinted, or reproduced without permission. Fair use is not easy to define, but the book publishing industry has some guidelines for navigating it and your copyeditor should know them well. Sometimes you can paraphrase, allude to, or attribute the source in ways that avoid the need to seek permission.

If you do decide that the lines of poetry, song lyrics, or a long passage from another writer are worth seeking permission to reprint, you will first need to identify the copyright holder. This may be a publishing house, record label, website, translator, songwriter, blogger, or author. Some will have online submission forms and others will require you to email or snail mail a letter requesting permission. You can find sample permissions letters online, but any format will require that you include information about their publication including the page number for the material you want to reprint.

In your request, you will need to give your title, price, publication month and year, press run quantity (which you can identify as print on demand), and format—whether paperback, hardcover, or e-book. Specify the rights you are seeking as "nonexclusive world rights, including electronic rights, to use this material as part of my work in all languages, for all editions, and in all media." There is a risk that they may only grant more limited rights than this, in which case you may run into trouble if you do things like sell foreign or translation rights, offer your novel as an audio book, or create future editions.

They will contact you with acceptable terms, perhaps their own contract for you to sign, and an amount you will need to pay. They may also include a few lines to document their rights grant that you will need to add—verbatim—to your copyright page. Read everything they send you carefully, because their terms could limit what you can do with the version of your book that includes their material.

If permission-seeking seems like a big deal, that's because it is. It is extremely important to navigate just right, and your copyeditor's assistance will be well worth paying for.

Process for Copyediting

There is not as much back and forth needed in copyediting as was possible in content-development editing. Unless you decide to do a sudden major revision—even just rewriting a paragraph is major at this point and highly discouraged—there will be only one round performed. The copyeditor will edit your entire manuscript using Microsoft Word's tracked-changes function, so you will see all corrections to the text and to the formatting. Step 7 showed you what these changes look like on screen. In the next section, you will learn how to use tracked changes to engage with your copyedited manuscript.

When the copyeditor is finished with their work, they will send you the tracked-changes version of the manuscript along with the stylesheet if your book requires one. It is then your turn to review the changes to be certain that they are workable and that they do not adversely affect your meaning, intention, or mistakenly cause confusion. Generally, only dispute changes that do one of these three things.

The most common experience authors have after reading through their copyedited manuscript is a sense of pleasure that the copyeditor made their writing truly shine forth. With problems writers didn't even know were there suddenly cleaned up, the sentences can read so effortlessly that they fall away as readers' imaginations go into high gear. The true goal of a great romance novel is that readers are so busy watching the movie running through their heads that they forget they are reading at all. A copyeditor can help that happen.

Using Tracked Changes

When you receive the copyedited manuscript, take a look through the pages to absorb how tracked changes works. The edits will all be in one color, with insertions underlined, deletions crossed out, passages that have been moved double-underlined, and highlighted passages connected to a comment bubble with a query or prompt typed inside. It's a good idea to go ahead and read all the comments so you can plan how to respond to them. You might be able to resolve the issues they point out straightaway, or they may take some thought.

Next, look at the top of your screen. In Microsoft Word, whether for PC or Mac, there will be a row of options like "File," "Home," and "Insert." These are known as tabs. Find the tab that says "Review" and click on it. The Review tab is where all the controls for the tracked-changes function are located.

The most important thing for you to locate on this menu is the button that simply says "Tracked Changes." If it is shaded, that means tracked changes are turned on. If not, tracked changes are off. Make sure that this button is shaded—meaning that it is turned on—and experimentally type into the manuscript.

You will notice that everything you type is a different color from the color that identifies the copyeditor's changes. This difference in color will help you create a full record of your work, and will eventually help the copyeditor see the work you have done. That way, they do not need to read through the entire manuscript again—instead, they can follow all your changes in your unique color. Now try experimentally deleting a word. It will change to your color and be crossed out.

On the Review tab, look for a button that says "New Comment." Next to it should be three more buttons with the same bubble icon: "Delete," "Previous," and "Next." These are the buttons you will use to navigate the copyeditor's comments. However, rather than using the Delete button to delete a comment, move your cursor to the copyeditor's comment bubble in the right margin and click on "Reply." If you have resolved a comment, type "Resolved" or "Done." If you want to say anything to the copyeditor, perhaps to explain something you did or didn't do, also click on Reply and type your comment into the extended bubble in the right margin. This way, you will maintain a complete record of your copyedit.

The same goes for the "Accept" or "Reject" buttons. You will not learn to use them here, because it is best for you to type directly over the copyeditor's changes if you want to alter, or even to revert, the edit.

It is a good idea to read through a manuscript twice when reviewing a copyedited manuscript: once while looking at all the copyeditor's changes, and once cleanly.

Read Cleanly While Tracking Changes

As you can see, looking at a document with marked-up changes in different colors can be very distracting and hard to read. So with your Tracked Changes button shaded to ensure that the function is on, go to the drop-down menu that says "All Markup." Click on the downward arrow and you will have the option of selecting "No Markup." By clicking on this view option, you can read a clean page and make changes that will be tracked in the background—even though you can't see them.

Copyedit Corrections

Once you have completed your review and have responded to all queries in comment bubbles, send the fully marked-up manuscript back to the copyeditor. They will review all your changes to make sure any new errors you have introduced get cleaned up. It's incredibly easy to make these errors, so assume that you will have added typos, style issues, and formatting snafus. The good news is that the copyeditor can easily fix them during the copyedit-corrections phase. They will then create a completely clean manuscript (with no tracked changes or comment bubbles) and send it to you.

Copyright Page

You will absolutely need a copyright page to identify you as the rights holder. It can be a good idea to ask for your copyeditor's help to create one. Here are common elements included on a self-published romance novel copyright page.

- Copyright symbol and year of publication, followed by either your name or the company name you are using to self-publish

- Copyright notice for the artist who did your cover illustration

- All-rights-reserved language, which has a variety of wording and depth that you can look up online

- Any disclaimers you want to make, whether about medical content, libel or likeness, violent or sexual content, or any others

- Credits for the cover and interior-pages designers

- Permissions grant-of-rights language

- Your personal publishing company's name, address, website

- Contact information to order books

- Edition number, which will need to be updated if you do subsequent editions

- Country where your book is being printed

- Print-run count, which is only applicable if you are printing in quantity rather than print on demand

Even if you create your copyright page yourself, since it's pretty straightforward, you still need someone to check it for clarity, formatting, and to remove any typos. And it will need to be in your final manuscript, so make it part of your copyediting process.

Final Manuscript

The version of your manuscript that you receive at this point is the only version you can call "final." The word actually indicates this: Absolutely no tinkering whatsoever! It is done, complete, and ready to be flowed into your interior-pages design.

True, this is not the last time you will be able to read through your novel and make any refinements. You will do so again, on a fully designed hard copy that has been printed out, at the proofreading stage. So if you do wake up in the middle of the night having realized there is some detail you simply must change, record it in a journal or notepad or text it to yourself, and hold onto it until you have reached proofreading stage.

Endorsements

If you want to seek endorsements for your romance novel, often this version of the final manuscript is the best one to send out as a .pdf or hard copy. You want your novel to read great for potential endorsers, but still have time in the schedule to put their endorsement on the cover before final files go to the printer.

There is some discussion about how effective endorsements truly are in influencing readers' buying decisions. So here you will only learn how to go about seeking endorsements if you wish to. Once you have a list of people who you want to ask to endorse your novel, write a completely personalized cover letter.

There should be little that is form-like about it. Here are some guidelines for what to include.

- Description of your connection with them

- Expression of admiration for their work

- Description of how your work relates with theirs

- Sales copy from the back of your book

- Timeline for them to send the endorsement a month after receipt of the manuscript

- A conclusion that suggests how they are contributing to their own work by supporting yours

- Your contact information, including a phone number

As you wait for their responses, remember that while it would feel really good to receive an endorsement full of praise, your success as a self-published romance novelist does not depend on it. Instead, there are so many ways to make your novel a success. One of them is to make the interior pages effortless to read.

To-Do Checklist

- ❑ Send your developed manuscript to the copyeditor

- ❑ Apply for permissions as needed

- ❑ Learn to use Microsoft Word's tracked-changes function

- ❑ Review the edits

- ❑ Respond to prompts and queries

- ❑ Send your reviewed and revised manuscript back to the copyeditor

- ❑ Receive the corrected and clean final manuscript with copyright page

- ❑ Send the final manuscript to potential endorsers

Flow Your Interior Pages

WITH THE FINAL VERSION of your manuscript in hand, it is ready to be flowed into the design you have chosen. If you have hired an interior-pages designer, ask them to create a sample layout for you to review and refine. A sample layout consists of the title page (the first page inside a book), table of contents, a chapter-opening page with the chapter number and title, and a few pages of text. If you have section breaks, make sure a couple of those are included in the sample.

As you learned in *Step 5: Learn New Skills or Hire Experts*, it can be a nice idea to carry the fonts used on the cover into the interior-pages design to offer readers a sense of continuity in the overall look. But this is not necessary, especially if you are purchasing a downloadable interior-pages template.

Beware of customizing an interior design too much. Readers have established expectations for how a romance novel should look, and just because you can tweak to your heart's desire doesn't mean you should. Here are some things to keep in mind.

Font Choice: Hopefully your interior-pages designer, or the designer who created your template, knows what main-text fonts make for effortless reading experiences and can choose one that conveys the overall tone of your book. As you review sample layouts or templates, try to sense what the main-text font is conveying: does it strike you as academic, impactful, playful, enchanting, artistic, soothing, edgy, sleek, futuristic? Then compare your impression to what tone matches your novel best, and see if they line up. If not, keep exploring until you find one that expresses the right tone, or one that is nice and neutral so that the emotional appeal is left up to your romance content.

Serif Font or Sans-Serif Font: Book fonts most commonly have serifs, which are tiny lines within the font style that actively guide readers' eyes horizontally across a line of text. This aids novel reading and can make the experience of absorbing a story easier. Serif fonts are therefore highly recommended. However, with the proliferation of online reading, sans-serif fonts have become more popular. These fonts look cleaner and more modern, but their clean lines stimulate readers' eyes to move vertically, which is better suited for scrolling through brief text on websites. When readers are deep into a novel, their eyes are more likely to grow fatigued with a sans-serif font. So as you consider which type of font to use in your self-published romance novel, decide whether a look conveying a sleek, modern tone is more important to you than readers' effortless experience—or vice versa.

Font Size: Font can indeed be too big, or too small, throwing off the fine balance between line spacing and text. Even a small increase in font size can also raise your page count, making the novel more expensive to print. One reason some readers choose e-books is that they can change the font size according to their preference. In print, however, it is better to choose a font size that is a happy medium—neither big nor small. If you are purchasing a template, choose one that comes with the font size you want rather than altering it manually, because doing so will hurt the delicate relationship between text and line spacing that aids readability.

Forms of Emphasis: Avoid using boldface, italics, and all-caps to emphasize something because they are distracting and interrupt readers' absorption in the book. It is likely that your editor already removed, or minimized, these. In romance novels, italics tend to be reserved to indicate a character's thoughts, conveying an inner conversation as opposed to the spoken words of dialogue within quotation marks.

Paragraph Indents: These are spaced according to a sense of balance with the width of the page. They work to lead readers into a fresh idea, theme, thought, pivot point, or line of dialogue, and really are essential in books. While online articles and blog posts do not indent paragraphs, reserve that flush-left style for online platforms. Indent the paragraphs in your book—even if you are going for a modern, futuristic, or sleek look.

Justified Text: When you justify your text, the lines in both margins are clean. It looks much tidier than ragged text on the right-hand side of the page—even though justified text occasionally breaks a word up onto two lines.

Word Breaks: Justified text is designed to make the most of the allotted space, and to do so the amount of spacing between words is altered automatically. Templates for the interior pages of books are programmed to increase this efficiency by occasionally breaking words up onto two lines, leaving a hyphen at the end of the line to indicate that the rest of the word is on the next line. Readers are quite used to this, as it is standard practice, so only concern yourself with word breaks if two or more are stacked on consecutive lines.

Chapter-Opening Pages: In book publishing, chapters always open on the right-hand page of the open book, which is known as the "recto" page. This is also true for title pages and the contents page. As your manuscript is flowed into the page layout you have selected, it may happen that the preceding chapter ends neatly on the opposite left-hand page, which is known as the "verso" page. But the preceding chapter may also end more awkwardly on the previous recto page instead. This leaves a blank verso page to fall opposite your recto chapter-opening page. Allow for this, as it is common in book publishing and readers are very used to it. Sure, it isn't an ideally efficient use of space to have a blank page, but it is preferable to altering word spacing in an attempt to "cheat space"—as you will soon read about.

Widows and Orphans: This is a quirky description for when a single word dangles on its own line at the bottom of a paragraph. It also indicates when a single line of text, left over from a preceding paragraph, opens a page. These things need to be avoided, for readability, looks, and adherence to book industry standards. Your interior-pages designer will be versed in this — as well as in ways to avoid it—but it is still something to be alert for. Templates will be programmed to automatically avoid them.

Altering Word Spacing: Occasionally a graphic designer or a programmed template will alter the word spacing to achieve things that are considered more important, such as removing word breaks or identical words that are stacked on two or more consecutive lines, avoiding widows and orphans, or working to end a chapter at a more desirable place. This may result in subtle—or obvious—variations in word spacing through the course of your novel. Some paragraphs may look tighter, others may look looser. Generally, cheating space like this is okay and readers will not notice any difference. But as you review your interior pages, it's a good idea to keep your eye out for any instances when paragraphs, pages, or chapters are glaringly too tight or too loose. If you are flowing your own novel, you may or may not be able to alter word spacing manually. It is extremely delicate work, so if you are very bothered by a variation in word spacing, you may want to hire a professional graphic designer to help you.

Create Your First Proof

Once the pages of your romance novel are designed, it is time to create the first proof. You will go through at least two rounds of proofs to read through your book in order to check all the layout considerations mentioned in this chapter, to truly polish in minor ways, to correct any egregious errors, and to fix all remaining typos.

Your graphic designer is likely to either send you a file in .pdf format so that nothing can be changed accidentally, or to print out and mail you a hard copy. If you flowed the interior-pages yourself, create a .pdf so that you have an electronic record. Be sure that you primarily relate with a version of the proof that is a two-page spread, so that it looks like an open book. This will most closely duplicate the eventual book-reading experience. This proof will be used by both you and your proofreader to polish the romance novel until it sparkles.

To-Do Checklist

- ❑ Choose an interior layout
- ❑ Flow the text into the design template
- ❑ Avoid too much customization
- ❑ Create the first proof

Scrub Errors with Proofreading

IT SHOCKS MANY AUTHORS to realize how different it is to read their romance novel after the interior pages have been designed. So far, you have been relating to it in manuscript form. After it has been flowed into book pages, things begin to feel real. It suddenly looks like a real book! This is a very exciting moment.

You and your proofreader can be reviewing at the same time, using your stylesheet (if your copyeditor found it necessary to create one) as the main guide. The secondary guide, which the proofreader will use so that you don't need to, is the *Chicago Manual of Style.*

In your initial negotiation with the proofreader, you can propose or ask how to handle the proofs. Will you email them a .pdf and they will have it printed? Or will you or your interior-pages designer have it printed, and then pop it in the mail or an express-delivery service? Either way works well.

Format for Printing Proofs

The proofs you and your proofreader review need to be two-page spreads so that pages look like an open book. You will want to read it at 100 percent of the intended size—don't shrink or enlarge it so you can review it at the exact same size that readers will. Since your book likely has a 6" x 9" trim size, all this means that you or your interior-pages designer will need to print it on 11" x 17" paper. It's not likely that your home printer will be capable of this, so definitely pay to have it printed at a retail office supply store or copy center. While you can print it double-sided to save a small amount of money, doing so makes it harder to keep pages in the right order and it is more challenging to go through than printing it single-sided.

Proofreading Symbols

There is a universal markup system for making corrections to your proof. Professional proofreaders will use it and your interior-pages designer will be able to read it so that they can make the corrections in the book's file. It's also important for you to learn it, and use it, so that everyone is communicating corrections in the same language. You can look up proofreading symbols online to find a cheatsheet to print and use as you read through your proof.

Tips for Proofreading Your Romance Novel

The time for content development has passed. You are finished with altering sentences in significant ways. Now is the time to catch any remaining errors. While, yes, you can refine things like word choice or comma placement, that is just about the most creativity you can apply at this point.

What you are looking for is anything that might embarrass you in print, and anything that got by the copyeditor—because it does happen. You are looking for things like these.

- Doubled words
- Formatting errors of any kind
- Identical words stacked in the layout
- Misplaced or misused punctuation
- Misspellings, especially with similar words

- Quotation marks and apostrophes that are not "smart," which means that they do not curl toward what they are enclosing, or perhaps they are curling in the wrong direction

- Style consistency in the layout and according to your stylesheet

- Typos of any kind

- Widows and orphans

- Word-break hyphens stacked on consecutive lines

When you spot any errors like these or of any kind, refer to your proofreading symbol cheat-sheet and mark up the proof accordingly. It's very helpful to use a brightly colored pen so that marks on the pages stand out easily amidst black text.

Collating Proof Markup

Once you have received the proofread proof back from your freelancer, it can be a good idea to collate your marked-up corrections onto their version of the proof. Here are some reasons for doing this.

- You can review their corrections as you collate and make any executive decisions about whether or not a change should be made

- Proofreaders will often have questions for authors, which they will likely write onto the proof, so collating gives you a perfect opportunity to address their queries

- Having everything on one proof will save you or your interior-pages designer time and effort as these corrections are typed manually into the book's computer file

Making Proof Corrections

With the proofread novel in hand, it is time to input the corrections into the book's computer file. Yes, this is done manually—one edit at a time—and it may or may not be time consuming. That depends on how clearly everyone marked corrections, how good you are at spotting the right place for making the correction in the computer file, and how extensive the proofread was. If you hired an interior-pages designer, simply send them the collated proof and they will input the corrections.

If you are inputting corrections yourself into a template, as you make larger corrections, like deleting a sentence for example, you will notice that the format automatically slides words around the page a bit. There will naturally be some shifting in the layout, which is one of the reasons you need to create a second proof.

The major reason for creating a second proof is human error. It is very easy to introduce additional errors as corrections are made. However careful you try to be, however concentrated you or your designer are on the task, you still need to double check everything.

Reviewing the Second Proof

Do not skip a second proof. Here are the things to look for when reviewing it.

- **Confirm that each change was made correctly.** To do this, take your first proof and lay it beside your second proof, going through pages one at a time, checking each correction as you do.

- **Check that no additional errors were introduced.** The only thorough way to do this is to read it again, and some authors hire a second proofreader—who has fresh eyes—to double check everything. Consider whether you might want to do this also.

- **Review the formatting on every page.** Do this in case the corrections caused the layout to slip enough to introduce something undesirable.

If you found any errors in your second proof, be willing to create a third, or even a fourth, proof. As long as you have any reason to be concerned about remaining errors, keep making proofs and follow the three tips for reviewing them offered in this section.

Proofreading Your Cover

You can ask the same proofreader to also review your cover. Even though you may have looked at it a thousand times, you may be blind to some typo, misspelling, or style mistake.

Approving the Final Proof

Your diligence in looking after details at proof stage can really pay off. It will help to create a romance novel that looks, feels, and reads wonderfully. So once you feel confident you have a clean-reading book on your hands, sign your name on the front page. This is your official sign-off, saying that your book is ready to go to the printer.

To-Do Checklist

❑ Print the two-page-spread proof on 11" x 17" paper

❑ Send the first proof to the proofreader so they work in tandem with you

❑ Find a proofreading symbol cheatsheet online

❑ Proofread your novel for egregious errors only

❑ Collate your work onto the proofreader's copy to streamline the corrections

❑ Make the corrections to the file yourself or give the marked-up proof to the designer

❑ Create a second proof

❑ Double check that all changes were made correctly

❑ Create as many proofs as you need to get things right

❑ Proofread your cover

❑ Sign the final proof to indicate it is approved

Get Final Files Ready to Print

IN ADDITION TO UPLOADING your final files to the printer's website, there are some requirements for self-publishing a romance novel that affect the book's life once you have finished creating it. Many of these can be addressed at any point in the publishing process but become essential when it's time for final files to go to the printer.

Assign an ISBN

An ISBN is the "International Standard Book Number" that retailers, online stores, and anyone in the book industry will use to refer to, or look up, your romance novel. Without it, your book will be adrift in the ocean. While it may be possible to purchase your ISBN through a print-on-demand company, you may prefer to assign your own through Bowker, the official ISBN agency in the United States. Visit their website to purchase one ISBN for your print book and one ISBN for your e-book.

After you buy the two ISBNs, which will each consist of thirteen numbers, you will be able to assign them to your print book and your e-book by filling out an online form. This form is incredibly detailed, since it covers all possible publishing possibilities, but it is fairly intuitive. Be sure to upload your front cover and fill in all the required fields. You can choose which other fields it would be nice to fill in for retailers and the book industry. When you are ready for the record to be live, simply click on that button. You can always go back into your record and make changes.

Generate a Barcode

With a barcode, when someone goes to purchase your romance novel in a bookstore, the person at the register just needs to scan the barcode and all the information you entered into Bowker's database will appear. You can either purchase a barcode to download from Bowker, or you can give your assigned ISBN to your cover designer and they will generate the barcode. It needs to go on the back cover of your novel, on the bottom right—lined up with the spine crease. Don't despair its ugliness, for it cannot be altered nor recolored in any way. Instead, regard your barcode as the book industry's stamp of legitimacy.

Choose Print on Demand

This book has approached the process of self-publishing your novel with the goal of printing on demand (POD). With the emergence, refinement, and now efficiency of POD technology, it is the most cost-effective way to print copies of your romance novel. Also, your book will never go out of print unless you intentionally take it off the market. And even after you have published the novel, you can make corrections, create a new edition, or change the cover by simply uploading new files.

How POD Works

When one person orders a copy of your book, POD will print one copy and mail it to them. This eliminates the need for self-publishing authors to warehouse large quantities of books, which they used to need to store in a dry place like a storage locker—or sometimes their living room! It also takes care of order fulfillment, so readers receive the copy they purchased in the mail.

Unless you want to undergo all the packing, addressing, and shipping hassle, POD is a much easier way to go.

Accounting

It used to be that POD was cost prohibitive—meaning it was a lot more expensive per book than printing say two-thousand copies at a bulk discount from a traditional printer. And yes, POD is still a bit more expensive per book. But considering how much time and trouble you save, it is more than worth it.

Another advantage to POD is that it reduces your up-front costs. Here's how the accounting works. Depending on how you set things up, when someone orders from Amazon, Barnes and Noble, or your own website, the order arrives at your chosen POD company. They take the money, subtract the cost for printing and shipping, and put the rest of the money in your royalty account. You can then withdraw that money at any time.

Here's a little bit of strategy, if you have just a small amount of time to devote to managing orders. Amazon, Barnes and Noble, and similar retailers will take a pretty significant chunk of the money you earn, similarly to the way they pay wholesale prices or take retailer discounts. So it will benefit you financially to create a marketing and publicity strategy that drives online buyers directly to you, and it can help to offer discounts for doing this. The money will go into your own account. Then you will order the copy to be printed and shipped to your buyer—paying the POD company to do so. So much more profit comes into your pocket without the middleman.

That said, it is still good to have a presence with the big online retailers. Many romance readers find new authors and novels using their search functions and "if you like that, maybe you will like this" enticements. Your POD company can help you set all this up, and may even help you open accounts with them.

Comparing Costs

When you are choosing a POD company, there may be an online form that will calculate the specific cost to print each book or you may need to request a quote. To calculate that, you will need to know the following.

- Your approximate, or preferably final, page count (which you will know at first-proof stage)
- What kind of paper you want (white or cream)
- Your trim size (most likely 6" x 9")

They can also tell you how much of a chunk the online retailers will take when they sell your book. POD companies are quite different and offer a wide variety of perks for using them. So do a lot of research when choosing which one to go with.

Order Samples

Go ahead and order sample books from the POD companies you are considering, so you can judge the quality for yourself—up close. Request samples with some variations: one copy with white paper and a gloss cover, and a second copy with cream paper and a matte cover. Then you can mix and match according to your preferences and to what best matches the tone of your romance novel.

Limitations of POD

It is important to be aware of the limitations of POD, so that you do not bump against them along the way. Here they are.

- Less paper choice
- No fancy cover treatments, like embossing or French flaps
- Less opportunity for color adjustment and press-checks on your cover

- If you add color to the interior pages, the cost goes way, way, way up

For romance novels, which have simple black and white interior pages, these limitations can be easier to navigate than for other kinds of books. And while it is true that POD may not duplicate your chosen shade of purple on your cover perfectly, the company should be willing to work with you until you are happier with it.

Preparing Final Files to Upload to the Printer

Here are the last touches that need to be done before your final files are ready to be uploaded to the printer.

Calculate the cover's spine width: Your printer will give you a formula that considers the paper weight and page count to calculate how wide the spine needs to be on your cover file.

Meet all the printer's requirements: Your printer should have these requirements available on their website, but if not, be sure to ask for them. The easiest way to meet them is to download one of their templates, with crop marks and bleeds, which will help you or your designer prepare the files for printing. You may need to adjust things like formatting, space between essential text or images and the trim line, image file size, and bleeds.

Create print-ready PDFs: You will upload two files: your color cover and then your interior pages as print-ready .pdf files. The interior pages will be single-paged (rather than the double-paged spreads you created for your proofs).

Order a Proof of the Printed Book to Review

It is essential to give the whole package one final review—especially to confirm that the right version was uploaded. That might seem obvious, but as you learned before, version control can be tricky and humans make mistakes. See how the color turned out on the cover and, if not perfect, consider whether it is acceptable. Glance through every page for glaring errors. You could read the novel again if you really want to, but at this point you might be too reader-fatigued to catch much anyway.

Then, when you are happy with your product, approve the files and celebrate!

To-Do Checklist

- ❑ Assign an ISBN
- ❑ Generate a barcode
- ❑ Prepare files for uploading to your print-on-demand company
- ❑ Order a proof of the printed book to review
- ❑ Make any needed changes to the files and re-upload them
- ❑ Approve the files and tell your printer to proceed with filling orders

Convert to E-Book Formats

WHILE THE MAJORITY OF romance novel readers prefer print books, many do like to use electronic devices. So reach your market within their reading preferences—whatever that may be—and convert to e-book formats. It is inexpensive to do even if you hire a freelancer, quite an easy process to learn, and well worth the money or effort. Here are some of the reasons romance readers like e-books.

- Text is reflowable, meaning it can change its flow so that it is optimized for any electronic device or program

- Readers can change the font size, font type, font color, and background color to match their preferences

- Engagement with the text is encouraged through the ability to bookmark pages, create electronic notes, and highlight passages

- Electronic libraries full of books are much easier to carry around, and easier to search, than printed libraries

Conversion Basics

You will use the print-ready .pdf file you uploaded to the printer to create your e-book formats. If you purchased an interior-pages template, simply follow the instructions for conversion that hopefully came with it.

There are two formats you will need to create so that your romance novel is available across all the popular, and even the less-popular, devices and e-readers.

> **Mobi Format:** This is the format that works for Kindle readers

> **EPub Format:** This format works for everything else, including tablets, computers, smartphones, and branded e-readers

Distributing Your E-Book

Your romance novel e-book will be widely distributed if you create accounts with two distributors: Amazon and Smashwords. Upload the .mobi file to Amazon for Kindle readers. Then upload the .epub file to Smashwords, where it will be distributed to reach many retailers including Apple iBooks as well as Barnes and Noble.

To-Do Checklist

❑ Convert your novel's file into .mobi and .epub formats

❑ Upload the files to distributors

You now have a self-published romance novel.

This is your champagne moment!

Share Your Love Stories with the World

THIS BOOK HAS WALKED you through the book-making part of the self-publishing journey. Hopefully you are thrilled with the feeling of holding your romance novel in your hand, and want to share it with others.

There are many online, in-person, and printed resources to help you with marketing and publicizing your book. Definitely make the most of them to sell your stories of love to the world. Then, when your next romance novel is ready to self-publish, return to this handy guide. The whole process gets smoother with repetition, and soon you will be on a roll to share the love.

To-Do Checklist

- ❑ Market and publicize your published romance novel
- ❑ Return to use this guide when it's time to repeat the process for your next novel
- ❑ Recommend this handy self-publishing guide to other aspiring romance authors

INDEX